PENGUIN
SPECIALS

Penguin Specials fill a gap. Written by some of today's most exciting and insightful writers, they are short enough to be read in a single sitting – when you're stuck on a train; in your lunch hour; between dinner and bedtime. Specials can provide a thought-provoking opinion, a primer to bring you up to date, or a striking piece of fiction. They are concise, original and affordable.

To browse digital and print Penguin Specials titles, please refer to **www.penguin.com.au/penguinspecials**

The Road Home

by

AI WEI

Translated from the
original Chinese

By Alice Xin Liu

PENGUIN BOOKS

UK | USA | Canada | Ireland | Australia
India | New Zealand | South Africa | China

Penguin Books is part of the Penguin Random House group of companies
whose addresses can be found at global.penguinrandomhouse.com

This paperback edition published by Penguin Group (Australia), 2019

1 3 5 7 9 10 8 6 4 2

Text copyright © Ai Wei, 2019

Translated from the Chinese by Alice Xin Liu

Produced with Writers Association of Zhejiang Province

Originally published in Chinese as *Hui Guxiang Zhi Lu* with the
Writers Association of Zhejiang Province and in People's Literature

The moral right of the author has been asserted.

Cover design by Di Suo © Penguin Group (Australia)
Cover illustration by Deng Yu © Penguin Group (Australia)
Text design by Steffan Leyshon-Jones © Penguin Group (Australia)
Printed and bound in China by RR Donnelley Asia Printing Solutions Ltd.

ISBN: 9780734398666

penguin.com.au

About the Translator

Alice Xin Liu is a writer and translator. She has worked as a news assistant for the *Guardian*, China Editor for *Index on Censorship*, editor at the Financial Times-affiliated *Danwei.org* (founded by Jeremy Goldkorn), and as Managing Editor of *Pathlight: New Chinese Writing*, with Paper Republic. Alice has translated two books and her freelance writings have appeared in *n+1*, *Granta, the Guardian*, Asymptote and other places. She is working on a novel. Alice also co-hosts the biweekly NüVoices podcast.

The Road Home

'What's wrong with you, Jiefang, you look like you have no energy.'

As mother was talking, Jiefang hung his head and didn't speak. He knew his mother knew what he was thinking, but the adults were always lying. It's been a day and a night since they took Daddy away. Jiefang was unsure why they had taken Daddy away.

Last night Jiefang went to the village head to take a peek at his father. Daddy was sitting underneath the dim light and there was no brightness in his eyes, he looked so nervous. Jiefang felt as if his father's soul had been split.

His Ma was now sitting inside their home's main room, picking through fresh soy beans; she was humming and hawing inside, instead of going to work. Jiefang knew that his Ma was waiting for his Pa.

Later when Jiefang walked into his classroom, he felt an uncertain air. He couldn't tell what was wrong.

Strongbull was bullying girls, the front of a pack of children, as he did normally. They were bullying a girl who had a long and thick braid, one just like Li Tiemei's. Strongbull also took a pull at the girl's plait. The girl steadied her braid and told Strongbull off. Both Strongbull and the boys laughed. Jiefang knew that Strongbull was actually interested in the girl. And of course Jiefang liked her as well. He liked her braid most of all. He really wanted to get a feel of the girl's long braid. He heard both Strongbull and his lackeys erupt in riotous laughter. Their laughter had a certain emotion behind it that day, thought Jiefang.

Radish was also laughing, off to one side; laughing harder than anybody else. This was how Radish always acted, and after he had enough of laughing he came to sit next to Jiefang. 'Your dad's still not home?' asked Radish.

Jiefang blushed and felt the violent pulsing beat of his heart.

'Don't you worry about it; your dad will be fine, he painted all those Mao portraits. Nothing will happen to him!'

Radish's words annoyed Jiefang. Jiefang had never hit anyone, but this time Jiefang screwed up his fist and directed it at Radish's nose without warning. Radish got a nosebleed. Radish didn't cry or shout out, but the shock was all over his face. Normally, before Strongbull would hit Radish, he would already be screaming his head off. This time Radish did not scream and blood just poured out of his nose. The classroom fell silent straight away and Strongbull was watching Jiefang with piercing eyes. Jiefang walked out of the classroom shouldering his backpack and with his head held high. Tears streamed down his face.

On the west side of the school was a row of mountains, and all sorts of plants and bird species abounded there. Jiefang went into the woods. He saw the sky in between the tree branches and shards of light ran alongside him. A while later he alighted next to a rock, which was his secret hiding place. There was a cocoon-space made out of the branches and the vines. Jiefang liked this place as soon as he saw it. And sometimes, he would take a nap there.

They could see the school through the lustrous leaves. They would already be in class right now–studying 'The Story of Huang Jiguan.' The students would be reciting the verses that the teacher had taught at the beginning of the year.

Back home, even though Daddy looked like he was concentrating on fixing the water bucket, he seemed absent-minded, which slowed down his movements. Ma was back, too, and she was at the stove. She must have found out about Jiefang not going to school today (their teacher was a good-for-nothing tattle-tale). If it was any other day, Jiefang would have gotten a good hiding, but today they didn't seem bothered by it. Jiefang didn't know what was different today.

*

The days passed. The house was quiet. They didn't take Daddy away again, but the oppressive atmosphere was still there. And Jiefang stopped thinking about the time they took father away.

The children in the school enjoyed the 'military lessons' the most. In the military lesson, the kids would learn the names of the different kinds of new weapons. The latest war was the Sino-Soviet border conflict, and the children found out a lot about Russian-style weapons: The T-54 tank, and the AK-47. The top of the T-54 tank was round, like a beautiful breast. The AK-47 could also automatically reload and shoot. The children were especially happy with the 'military lessons' in the woods during every semester. The class was taught simulated warfare. The students were split up into a few small teams, and sent to look for the already-buried paper notes the teachers had placed under the stones or the near the tree-trunks or are on the branches. The notes read the following: 'Enemy Commander,' 'Enemy Army Commander,' 'Enemy Division Commander,' and 'Enemy Soldier,' etc. The student who could get the most notes was the hero.

The skies were clear and bright; early summer had arrived, and the sun, once it hit the body, made a faint pain. The students who had military uniforms put them on (many of the students had gotten their parents to make child-sized military uniforms for them two months prior), with a belt securing their attire.

The students wearing uniforms had a layer of sweat because of how hot it was, and their faces were as red-coloured as the sun. The students who wore shirts always looked the freshest.

The students were feeling edgy as they waited. They were waiting for the teacher to make the call of general attack so they could run into the woods to capture their enemies. The air inside the woods was cool and damp, with the earthly compound added to it. Their sweat would retreat back into itself once they entered the woods.

The students discovered a ditch two-thirds down the ubac. They were in wonderment. They thought that perhaps this was a trench. There were luxurious trees growing both in front of the ditch and behind it. But there were some weeds that grew on top of the ditch that were taller than its banks.

The children didn't know how deep the ditch was so they jumped down, and their lower bodies were annihilated within the weeds. They ran along the ditch excitedly. The weeds were everywhere underfoot. The sun was beating down fiercely, and not a minute later, the weeds stamped down underfoot had lost their original green lustre, wilting. The children belly-crawled in the trench, like they had seen soldiers do in the movies, and imitated the sounds of cannons, grenades and machine guns. After a while, the teacher showed up at the ditch. A few of the children came together around the teacher to ask why the trench was there?

'There was a ferocious war that happened here before the Liberation,' replied the teacher. 'The Kuomintang were over there, on the mountain, and the Liberation Army was here. At the time the KMT planes flew all over above us, and hit us on the mountains with bombs.'

The stories made the children surge with excitement. This military lesson had just taken on the feeling of a real war. It was as if what they captured – the battalion, the regiment leader – weren't just pieces of paper, but real people.

The smell of gunpowder entered Jiefang's nostrils. Jiefang hadn't just imagined this from listening to the teacher; he really did smell gunpowder. Jiefang had the best sense of smell out of everyone. Jiefang thought that the smell of gunpowder was the best smell in the whole world; all of the pores on his body opened up after he smelled gunpowder and his whole being relaxed. He wondered where the gunpowder smell came from.

Radish found a bullet in the middle of the wild weeds and started to shout excitedly.

The news that a bullet was picked up in a trench on the mountains spread like wildfire through the village. The children would rush there after school or on Sundays just like the incoming tide. They would come with shovels and pickaxes and they dug and dug in the trench, looking for bullets or shells. Any student who found one would be admired by all those around.

Jiefang put his nose down on the trench's ground like a dog. He would dig down wherever he smelled the whiff of gunpowder and would find a bullet. Jiefang got more bullets and shells than anyone else. His bullets clinked against one another in his backpack, which was strapped to the front of his chest. The others were all jealous of him. Radish was so impressed by Jiefang's sense of smell and was extremely willing to help Jiefang dig when he smelled the scent of a bullet.

'Let me help you dig,' Radish would say, 'I can't find bullets anyway, I'm just being modest, like the soldier Lei Feng.'

Jiefang agreed to the proposition.

To get to the bullets underneath the ground, Jiefang tore up his hands, and his fingernails were mutilated with both hands marked with bloody scabs. Except Jiefang didn't just use Radish; he would also occasionally gift him with a bullet. When Radish held the bullet in his hand, a sweet, dreamlike smile would spread across his face.

Radish suddenly told Jiefang as he was helping him dig one day, 'Jiefang, Strongbull said your father had made a mistake and is going to be purged. He drew *Dong Cunrui Blows Up The Bunker* underneath a painting of Chairman Mao. They said that your father had bad intentions. He wanted to blow up our Great Leader, Chairman Mao.'

This grated on Jiefang. He leapt up, and had Radish by the collar. He said, 'Fuck your mother. What are you talking about? Why would Dong Cunrui blow up Chairman Mao?'

'It's the truth, Jiefang. They are all saying it. Haven't you felt it? They don't play with you anymore.' Radish looked sincere.

Jiefang let go of his collar and sat down on the floor. He thought, *Radish's right; they are avoiding me. Even though I used to be a loner, kids still wanted to play with me, and now they just stare at me from afar, like I am some kind of monster.*

Jiefang had been confused for a while. Now that Radish spoke out, he knew the reason. Jiefang understood. *This was a huge rumour about his Daddy making this mistake,* thought Jiefang, *how could Dong Cunrui possibly blow up Chairman Mao?* Also, he was the one who asked Daddy to add the painting of Dong Cunrui.

How could my Daddy be so ill-intentioned that he would want to blow up Chairman Mao? There must be someone who is spreading this rumour, and Jiefang suspected that it was Strongbull. *Strongbull is the real baddie; he wants to bully everybody, but he doesn't dare bully me, and so he makes up these rumours.* Jiefang decided that he had to respond to Strongbull in some way.

Strongbull stood up and glanced to the south of the trench, a group of children were horsing all around Strongbull and one was even fanning him. Jiefang started to panic, as he knew that Strongbull was not someone he wanted to provoke. Strongbull had a cruel and merciless streak, and was capable of anything.

Radish had been watching Jiefang and felt the tense atmosphere in the air. Radish knew what Jiefang wanted to do– he knew about his temper. Radish said, 'Forget it, Jiefang. There are so many of them.'

'I'm not afraid of him–how could I be, I'm not even afraid of death!'

Jiefang looked pale, but he was steely and determined. *I also have to respond. Even if I can't win in a fight with Strongbull, I still have to respond. I'm not afraid of anything, not even death. I would have been a hero if I were born when we were at war.*

As Jiefang had these thoughts, he had already come to stand next to Strongbull. Jiefang stood still about three meters away from Strongbull as he saw him become vigilant, a smile freezing on Strongbull's face. Jiefang waved to Strongbull, asking him to come over. Strongbull walked over with his face full of disdain. Jiefang didn't say anything, but instead, he threw a punch directly at Strongbull's face. When he hit out with his punch, both his legs shook uncontrollably. He felt the listlessness of the punch that he threw like he had just come out of a huge illness, with no strength left. It was obvious that Strongbull didn't expect Jiefang to do this. Strongbull felt a twinge in his nose, and when wiping it with his hand, he saw the redness of blood. Strongbull screamed out and lunged towards Jiefang. So the two of them became entangled, both wanting to conquer the other. The other children were confused by this sudden battle and they watched as the two fought, not knowing whether they should get involved or stop it. Both of the fighters were on the ground now, rolling around; first Jiefang was on top of Strongbull, and next Strongbull was on top of Jiefang, and both of them were heavily out-of-breath.

They didn't speak when they fought. Normally when children fought there would be a stream of swearwords. The other kids, watching from the side, were so nervous they couldn't breathe. There were sounds of two people's hands, feet, and bodies fighting in the air. Then the two got up from the ground and took hold of each other's clothes and hair, making circles up and down the hills.

Jiefang had no more strength left and moved completely according to routine. *I'm going to lose the battle if I continue like this,* he thought.

Spontaneously, Jiefang opened his mouth and bit Strongbull's shoulder. Strongbull shouted 'Ah!' and lifted his head, thrashing it on top of Jiefang's head. They both fell to the ground at the same time and like two rocks they rolled down the mountain. The children started to run down the hill towards them – when they got there, Jiefang and Strongbull were no longer fighting but moving in opposite directions. Jiefang was going south, whereas Strongbull was going north. There was blood on Strongbull's white shirt.

Radish seemed to have a lot on his mind. To Jiefang he said, 'Jiefang, Strongbull said he will always chase you. Strongbull said you have no morals, he said you bit him; you almost snapped the tendons in his shoulder. He said only rabid dogs bite. If you were human, you would use your hands and feet to fight, not your mouth. Jiefang, you ought to be careful. Strongbull said he's going to bite you next time as well.'

Jiefang laughed coldly.

'He wouldn't dare,' he said. 'If he spreads another rumour about Daddy, I'll never let him live it down.'

Despite his words, Jiefang was still worried. He didn't want to fight Strongbull anymore. He couldn't guarantee that he would be able to win against Strongbull next time. Strongbull also had so many lackeys and if they stepped in, Jiefang wouldn't be a match for him. Over the next few days, Jiefang tried to avoid coming into unavoidable confrontation with Strongbull.

*

Explosions sounded now and again in the village. Explosions they may have been, but they were not that loud, although they really were louder than firecrackers. This was a new game invented by the children: the bullets they collected went into a burning firepit and the bullets would explode. The fire would look like it was being blown by a gust of wind when the bullets exploded; it would look like it would distinguish, but immediately it would be set aflame again.

Strongbull had already forgotten about fighting with Jiefang and was entranced by the game with the exploding bullets. Strongbull also thought of a new idea: He laced a bullet on the foot of a tortoise and threw the tortoise into the fire. The tortoise was blown into two as the bullet exploded. The half with the head was still alive after the blast.

There wasn't much of a store of bullets left, so Strongbull went to collect the bullets from other children. But the bullets had but all finished exploding after a while and only shells were left.

The children knew that Jiefang had quite a few bullets. Jiefang actually had the most bullets out of everyone in the village. But Jiefang didn't play the exploding bullets game. Jiefang didn't want to copy Strongbull, even if he was determined to play this game.

They can go right ahead and play, thought Jiefang. *They'll discover quickly that I am the only one in the village who has genuine bullets. They will be jealous of me soon enough.*

Jiefang made sure that the bullets in his bag jangled as he walked along. He still saw deep evil intent from the look Strongbull threw over at him sometimes. *The eviler his looks, the more jealous he is of me,* thought Jiefang.

An outsider suddenly arrived in the village. He said he was a cadre from the People's Armed Forces Department. He started looking for Strongbull as soon as he got to the village. It wasn't long before they brought Strongbull in front of the outsider.

When the person from the People's Armed Forces Department saw Strongbull, he directly asked him to hand over his bullets. 'We've been told that you'd picked up plenty of bullets, and you let them explode, including on the ass of a passer-by. Hand over the bullets–did you know that keeping bullets is against the law? You can go to jail,' he said to him.

Strongbull smiled. He had no bullets left; they had

all become shells, with a loud pang! 'I don't have any bullets, not even one. I'm not lying to you–they have all exploded. But I do know who has hidden away bullets, I'll take you to him,' said Strongbull.

Strongbull led the cadre from the People's Armed Forces Department towards Jiefang's house. Jiefang was standing underneath a chinaberry tree in his court-yard, unmoving. *What were the People's Armed Forces Department cadres doing here? Were they here to take Daddy away again?* Jiefang was so worried that some-thing worse had happened to Daddy. He saw Strongbull point over in his direction, speaking to the People's Armed Forces Department, then stopping. The cadre came towards him with an exaggerated swagger. The eyes of the outsider stabbed him like claws. Jiefang's heart started to beat faster. His face was flushed as if he was drunk with wine.

So the cadres from the People's Armed Forces Department were here to collect bullets. Jiefang breathed a sigh of relief. Jiefang knew that Strongbull would have told the outsiders that he had bullets and he couldn't deny it. Even though he didn't want to, Jiefang spilt the things in his bookcase on to the floor with ease and a whole bunch of bullets rolled out. 'They're all here,' he said. 'Take them.'

Jiefang didn't give up all of his bullets. He still kept five. He hid the five bullets underneath a piece of a stone board behind his house. He would take out the five bullets from underneath the stone tablet when his parents were not there. It was all he could do to stop himself from shooting these bullets at Strongbull.

The kids in the countryside were spreading the rumour that Jiefang was going to seek his revenge on Strongbull. Strongbull will pay for his informant ways.

Radish's heart rate shot up when he heard about this, *If the two of them fought, someone is going to get hurt.* He ran to Jiefang, out of breath. 'Jiefang, are you really going to fight Strongbull?' He asked.

Jiefang didn't answer. The smile on his face was one of condescension as if he had already defeated Strongbull.

'Jiefang, provoking Strongbull is not a good idea. He was still looking to get your back for the time you bit his shoulder,' Radish continued.

Strongbull had heard the same rumour about Jiefang's revenge mission and his mood changed completely. 'Let him try. I'll show you all! There will be a day when he'll be on the ground begging for mercy,' he said.

Neither one of them made the move to provoke the other. Jiefang spent his time alone. Sometimes Radish would follow behind Jiefang (Radish followed Strongbull more often, but Strongbull insisted on mocking him), while Strongbull would roam the village with a group of kids. It was as if the two of them had a secret understanding; they would miss each other on their walks.

But the village was too small. Finally, one day, Jiefang and Strongbull met in the middle of a small alleyway. The alleyway was deep, about fifty metres. White saltpeter lined the bottom of the walls on either side of the alleyway. Jiefang knew that white saltpeter could be used to manufacture dynamite.

After Strongbull saw him, he stood still at the other end of the alleyway. Perhaps nothing would have happened if Strongbull hadn't moved or if he had strolled over casually. But now Strongbull stood still, and the kids behind Strongbull did the same.

Strongbull's expression looked extremely serious and he followed Jiefang closely with his gaze. Jiefang didn't stand still, rather he continued to walk towards the other end of the alleyway. He didn't look over at Strongbull and only concentrated on the white saltpeter at the bottom of the wall. He could smell dynamite. He sensed that his day had finally arrived. Perhaps now was the opportunity to see who would come out on top – he or Strongbull.

Jiefang fantasized about the white saltpeter on the bottom of the walls turning into dynamite, with which he would blow up this entire alleyway. Of course, it wouldn't be possible. Jiefang put his head down, and said to himself, 'Everything is up to you now.' He tried his best to brush away his fear and walked towards Strongbull as if he had nothing on the line.

When he went past Strongbull, Strongbull stopped him in his tracks. 'Hold up. I heard you wanted revenge?' he asked.

Jiefang stopped walking. He didn't need to; he could have quickened his pace and walked away. But if he did that, not only would Strongbull look down on him, but everyone else would too and he would become the target of everyone's bullying and mockery, just like Radish. Jiefang was immovable in front of Strongbull, as if his foot was nailed down to the floor. It was the first time his gaze pierced Strongbull and Strongbull felt the decisiveness of his gaze, which panicked him. At this point, there was nowhere for Strongbull to go. 'I'm in front of you now,' he said. 'You wanted revenge? Come get it.'

Jiefang looked at the kids behind Strongbull, and sneered. 'Do you need all these people to protect you against me?'

'I don't. It'll just be you and me—don't you worry.'

'One on one. Fine. How do you want to do it?'

'You decide.'

Jiefang thought about it. 'We have fought already with our fists. Let's do a mud fight this time.'

Mud fights were a particular type of game for children. Each side created their stations on either side of the same area, used mud like cannonballs and whoever was able to surpass the middle won. But it was obvious now that it was no longer just a game, it was real war.

Strongbull glanced at Jiefang with alertness; he wanted to know what tricks Jiefang was up to. Strongbull thought that there was cheating involved and that perhaps Jiefang would use a lethal weapon against him.

Jiefang's proposal really meant that they were now going from a fist fight into an armed battle. They came to dry, cracked mud land near the Eastern side of the village. It used to be a shallow lake, but it hadn't rained for a long while, so it was now a dehydrated, split mud land.

Jiefang and Strongbull started to prepare for war. Jiefang's pockets were full of mud pies. Some of them were as hard as rocks. He hoped that these mud rocks would be aimed square on Strongbull's face. *I can't lose no matter what. If I lose this time, then I might lose ten times, or one hundred. I have to pass the middle line before Strongbull, even if I am killed by him.*

Jiefang and Strongbull both looked for a hidden place to belly crawl down. The kids who were watching hid nearby on a stretch of grass. 'Begin!' screamed one child. Before he even finished speaking, mud balls started shooting towards each other from the boys' respective positions.

If this was a normal war, the firepower at the beginning would be thick and fast, and an attack would be hard. When there's less firepower and the mud balls on both sides have been used up—that's the best time to charge artillery.

But Jiefang's actions shocked everybody; he attacked from the start. He didn't even throw his mud balls to the other side. He passed through the rapid firepower and the mud cakes hit him one by one, and even when he was down, he got up immediately and kept attacking. The kids watching thought Jiefang had lost it. So it was no surprise when a mud cake flew into Jiefang's eyes and they immediately swelled up like a bun.

His vision was blocked by the swelling. Jiefang wasn't sure what direction he was going in now. At the same time, his foot hit something and he somersaulted to the ground. Strongbull saw his opportunity, and so he came out from his hiding place and ran towards the middle.

Jiefang saw this and he quickly got off from the floor. He smiled from one corner of his mouth. He took out the mud cakes from his pocket and smashed them towards Strongbull. Strongbull was hit so forcefully he landed on the mud. When he was able to get up again, red-blooded hate had pierced both his eyes and in his hands was a rock the size of his fist. According to the rules, they were not supposed to use rocks, yet Strongbull was holding one. If he hit Jiefang with it, he would surely lose his life. The kids watching the war were nervous and their faces turned pale.

Strongbull really did make the move to throw the boulder towards Jiefang and used all of his energy to hurl it in his direction. The rock was like a rain-day cloud, passing over the children's eyes. They closed their eyes because they didn't want to look anymore. The rock hit Jiefang's head. It wasn't long before Jiefang's face was bloodied, and his head was sprouting blood, too. But Jiefang wasn't beaten. He stubbornly continued to run towards the middle line. Strongbull was shocked, he didn't think the rock would really hit Jiefang. He saw a blood-head running towards him and instantly felt fear. He cried out, *'Ahhhh!'* and ran away. The kids knew that they had overdone it and so they ran as well.

Jiefang didn't know what happened next.

*

Strongbull knew he was in great trouble. He hid on the mountain and didn't want to go home. He knew his parents would kill him if they found out. Later a friend had come up the mountain to say that Jiefang had passed out soon after reaching his home and now was in the town hospital. He said that Jiefang might die. Upon hearing this, Strongbull was so scared and yet he knew that he had to face the consequences this time. He gritted his teeth and went home. There, his parents tied him to a tree and beat him terribly. After they beat him, they went to the town to pay for all of Jiefang's medical fees. They did not untie Strongbull when they left.

Strongbull hung on the tree, and thought, If Jiefang

died, then I would have to die, too. He knew the simple truth of an eye for an eye. He couldn't stop himself from shaking, and the rope from which he hung also shook.

When Strongbull's parents came back from the hospital, he had already fainted from his fear. His parents cut him down from the rope, woke him and said, 'Jiefang is alive.'

After a few days, the parents took Strongbull to the hospital to make amends with Jiefang. His parents told him, 'Jiefang had a brain injury and he can only smile. He smiled at everyone — we don't know if he is a moron now. If he is, then we would be responsible for him his whole life.'

Strongbull stopped speaking for a while, he knew it was better to stay silent. They arrived at the hospital, but Jiefang didn't want to see Strongbull, so Strongbull stood just outside the door. *So he's not an imbecile,* Strongbull thought, *He still knows that I'm his nemesis.* He looked inside, and he saw that Jiefang was indeed smiling, but his eyes were not smiling. It was obvious that he was trying hard to stop himself but was having a hard time, and that was the rage in his eyes. Strongbull was suddenly overcome with pity for Jiefang, *What isn't pitiable about someone who only knows how to smile?*

Jiefang still smiled when he left the hospital. He couldn't stop himself. He didn't want Strongbull to see him like this. In front of Strongbull, he persevered to control his expression, but instead of relaxing his facial muscles, he was in between laughter and tears. He knew that this was uglier than smiling and he felt utterly hopeless. After a while of working on his expression, the expression would change, too. He started looking as if he was pretending to smile, which made him look like he was extremely clever but also an idiot. Of course, Jiefang was unhappy with the expression he saw on his face. He couldn't stand the looks which the villagers gave him; they were looks of pity, and at the same time, as if they were looking at a monster. Jiefang now rarely stayed in the village and instead would go to the mountains. What was strange to Jiefang was that he wouldn't smile his idiotic smile when he was alone. Nobody in the village knew what Jiefang was doing on the mountain.

The smell of gunpowder was always in Jiefang's brain. Since the time they found those trenches, he could feel the smell of gunpowder in his brain. This scent had gotten stronger after Jiefang was struck. Jiefang told his mother this and as she listened she started to cry. After he saw his mother cry, Jiefang stopped telling her these things.

Jiefang also told Radish, but Radish simply said it was his imagination, 'The bullets on that other side of the trench had been dug and taken away completely. Why would there be the scent of gunpowder? It would be good if there really was gunpowder; the villagers wanted to cut into the mountain and couldn't find any gunpowder. All the gunpowder had been confiscated by the State for the production of rockets.'

But Jiefang could smell gunpowder all the same.

The children didn't go over to play by the trench anymore because there were no more bullets to find there anymore, yet Jiefang went there daily. When he stood on top of the trench, the familiar smell of gunpowder would enter his nostrils by force. He would, at this point, run around near the trench like a drunkard. This euphoria would temporarily soothe his troubles.

One day, when he was running in the woods, Jiefang tripped over and landed heavily. He landed on a fallen tree and there was blood on his elbow. He saw that a piece of metal had tripped him up. Jiefang was suddenly inspired: his foot had discovered something amazing. It was always like this; sometimes you discovered things with your eyes, and at other times you had to use other body parts. Jiefang knew that his fall wasn't for nothing, it was so he could find an even deeper secret underneath the piece of metal. Was it a bomb? A mine? An armoured car? It was a bomb.

Jiefang saw it after digging for five nights.

*

The last school lesson always ended at three in the afternoon. He would run into the mountains as soon as he was out of the classroom. Of course, he wasn't going to tell anyone that he had found a bomb. The sun had set over the mountain on the opposite side of him and he could see the hues of blood-red dusk–it coloured the bomb in a layer of faint red, too. This was an enormous bomb; even though it had been in the ground for 20-odd years, it looked just like it was fresh out of the shop room in a weapons factory. Apart from particular areas that had rusted where the paint had chipped off, silver still glowed from other parts.

Its model was written on the tail-end of the bomb, except you couldn't quite see it anymore. Jiefang guessed that this was probably an American-made bomb–it was one that the Americans had offered Chiang Kai-shek to fight the Civil War. The bomb was as long as a fully-grown adult and its diameter was the same as a water bucket. Jiefang forcefully pushed the bomb, but he couldn't move it. *This bomb hadn't yet exploded*, thought Jiefang, *there is a ton of gunpowder inside, I bet*.

No matter what, this was a significant discovery. For the moment, Jiefang didn't want to tell anyone. *I have to understand it completely first and then I can figure out everything else.*

Jiefang hid the bomb well before coming down from the mountain. He covered the bomb with grass, vines, and firewood until he knew that no one would find it, then he left peacefully.

His heart was in the mountains as he sat in the classroom. It flew to where the huge bomb was. Occasionally he would skip class to go up the mountain, but not often enough that the teacher would tell the students to go look for him on the mountain. He was scared that if they did, they would find out that he had found a bomb. Jiefang couldn't stop himself from looking out the window, the blue outside the window was like painted glass. Jiefang had once found a piece of painted glass and when he used it to look at the world, the world became wondrous; it was as magnificent as a fairytale.

Jiefang would look out the window for a long time and a different kind of mysterious smile would appear at the corner of his mouth. Of course, the teacher knew that Jiefang's attention had wandered, but many people said that his brains were bad because of Strongbull, and so the teacher didn't bother with Jiefang. Even though Jiefang didn't look at the blackboard and didn't listen, at least he was quiet.

Because of the mud incident, Strongbull was moved to another class. The teacher was of the opinion that letting the two of them sit together in class was like burying a ticking time bomb in the class—it could explode at any moment. Strongbull was happy to go to another class as he didn't want to be in conflict with Jiefang.

Even though the doctor said there have been no injuries to Jiefang's brain, everyone said that he was pretty stupid now.

It didn't matter whether Jiefang was stupid or not, it was a matter of the smack that Strongbull had thrown. Strongbull felt bad about it. After he had been moved to another class, the teacher said that Strongbull had become quiet and no longer took a group of kids around bullying others. Some said that Strongbull had begun to do good.

One afternoon, the school put on a 'Remember the Past to Savor the Present' assembly. When the children heard about this assembly, their stomachs started growling, because they'll soon eat bran pancakes. Bran was usually used to feeds pigs, and these pancakes showed the children that in the old society, workers were no better than cows, pigs or horses. The pancakes were now used to engender feelings of happiness from the inner depths of the children in the new society. Except the children didn't like eating bran pancakes, they thought that the taste was bitter, even though they had a fragrance that made you drunk. Then the children also discovered that the pancakes used for 'Remember the Past to Savor the Present' had flour mixed into them, so that they would eat them. Hence, they now treated these pancakes as a pleasure for their bellies.

The children sat happily in the auditorium waiting

for the people giving the presentation. In a moment, the balding principal and another man, who looked like a skeleton, came on the stage. When they saw him, commotion swept through the crowd. He was so frightening-looking. There were scars all over this man's face: He had no ears; no eyelids, and there were only eye-whites when he shut his eyes. He also had no visible skin, with only the inner layer of his skin, completely smooth and without pores, on his body.

The principal asked for silence, and then introduced the person with panache. His name was Mei Long, and he used to live here, but now he worked in the grain shop in town. He hadn't been home for a very long time and the children no longer recognised him. This person was a model worker and his face was blown up by a bomb when they were building the dam during the Great Leap Forward. The children didn't dare look at him when the principal introduced him. And you could guess the expression on Jiefang's face.

Jiefang actually really wanted to know the story with the model worker, for example how he got to be this way. Except he knew that he wasn't here for that; he was only here to complain about the sad lives of the workers in the old society. Jiefang was, to some extent, disappointed. The person started to speak, and the eyes which had no eyelids cried tears because he was unable to blink. Normally this may only have been a failing, but during the presentation, it had an unimaginable effect. The images of life in the old society, recounted in his tears, caused the listeners' sorrow and many kids cried with Mei Long. These were honest tears. The lives of workers under the order of the old society was so hard—the landlords and rich peasants really were evil. The children felt class hatred in their hearts.

Some of the children directed their gaze towards the students whose family were landlords and rich peasants. The children of these 'four sinister elements' lowered their heads, and hid them inside their chest cavity, it looked as though their heads grew from there. These 'four sinister elements' cried harder than anyone else and some shook uncontrollably because they knew that physical beatings awaited them after the presentation was over. The class hatred and rage that had been ignited in the children will be unleashed on them.

It was always like this. When the presentation finished, the children would encircle the sons and daughters of the 'four sinister elements,' and enact violence towards them.

Jiefang kept his gaze on the person on the stage.

He was imagining what kind of heroic feats this man, who had a face of scars, had accomplished. *How could he call himself a hero, looking the way he did*, thought Jiefang, *I could present on the stage, I am qualified, and I should enjoy the endless stream of applause.*

Strongbull sat in a corner that was far away from Jiefang. He watched Jiefang the whole time. He couldn't help but watch him. His gaze went across the top of the crying children and projected onto Jiefang's face. Jiefang still had that strange smile and his Adam's apple, which appeared sometimes, moved up and down now and again, as if he were swallowing and from his eyes, a strange glow emanated. Suddenly, Jiefang stopped smiling (but could only do this temporarily) and his sharp gaze went towards Strongbull. Strongbull looked away quickly so that he didn't have to intersect his gaze with Jiefang.

Even now, as long as Strongbull's gaze stayed on Jiefang for more than half a minute, it didn't matter if the gaze was on Jiefang's back or on Jiefang's side, Jiefang would respond angrily. Jiefang acted as if Strongbull'sstare was full of darts that could pierce and hurt his skin. Jiefang saw that Strongbull's gaze hurriedly flashed somewhere else. He expected no good intentions from Strongbull.

Jiefang had seen a Vietnamese film called *Duong Ve Que Me*. There was a soldier, on his way home, who slept inside a bomb. This was how he managed to avoid a passing US fight-plane. This scene had stayed with Jiefang. He wanted to be like that soldier, sleeping inside the shell. He could imagine there and then the warm feeling of the slumber. Jiefang imagined the bomb in front of his eyes; the twilight light bouncing off its smooth outer streamlined shell, making it look beautiful in its stillness. Jiefang knew that the stillness was only on its exterior, he knew that gunpowder filled it on the inside, and if ignited, a big cut would be blown into the mountain.

Now it was shut tight, so you couldn't find a crack, and it was as round as an egg, as if it were like this naturally. Jiefang knew that it was made by workers in a military factory, piece by piece. It could be taken apart with some thinking. Jiefang remembered a huge piece of metal at the tail-end of the bomb and he knew that all the mechanisms were in there.

*

When he went to the mountain, Jiefang brought a screwdriver, hammer, pliers, spanner and other tools from his home. He had decided to start from the tail-end of the bomb to take the bomb apart into two. Then he would be able to sleep in the bomb just like the Vietnamese soldier.

Even though the bomb didn't explode when it dropped down from the skyand even though it has been in the ground for more than twenty years, disassembling it was undoubtedly dangerous work. Jiefang didn't know under what circumstances the bomb would explode; he had no knowledge in this respect, but he decided to take the risk. Jiefang held up the screwdriver to pick away at the bitumen at the end of the bomb. A screw-nut came out immediately. Jiefang knew that he had to screw out the screw-nut. His heart beat like crazy as he was doing this, he was worried that he would accidentally make the bomb go off, and be blown to smithereens. Perhaps, they wouldn't even be able to find a bone.

After he got rid of the nut, he could remove the back cap. There were some red and green wires inside. This scenario was very familiar to Jiefang–the movies showed this scene all the time. The common high point in all films was always when the bomb was about to explode and the hero of the story was at their most desperate moment. The camera always captured this dire situation, when sweat beads the size of peas would gather on the hero's forehead as they were trying to decide which wire to cut first, the red or green one. Of course, the hero would never let the bomb explode, courage and luck would save them.

Jiefang thought that he was accomplishing something amazing, as if he had become the hero now. But this feeling was fleeting. There was no smoke; the mountains, the trees, the sunset were completely peaceful. There seemed to be no potential threat. He was worried, when he started, that the bomb would explode suddenly, but when there was no movement with the bomb after a while, his feeling of danger dampened. Jiefang looked at the wires inside the bomb and felt like they were only there for decoration. Jiefang did not think about it as he grabbed the bunch of them and pulled with might. The cords left the bomb. The bomb did not explode.

Jiefang got bolder and bolder, and his speed at disassembling the bomb got faster and faster. At last, he opened the shell of the bomb and the shell split in two. There was a ball of black-something that was enclosed in an oily and dirty paper, and Jiefang guessed immediately that it was gunpowder. He had read a description of it in a book about military affairs and its official name was TNT.

The ball was the most astounding thing; the bombshell was but the coat for this ball. The ground and the mountain would shake if it went off. In order to settle it, Jiefang went down the mountain and found the paint barrel that his father used to paint the portrait of the Leader. There was paint inside and on the outside of the barrel, and Jiefang lit it on fire so that the barrel would burn until all of the paint was gone.

He knew that fire could not go near gunpowder, so he immersed the metal bucket in water before he took it back up the mountain. He used his shirt to wipe away the water in the barrel.

After he arrived on the mountain, he put the ball of black gunpowder into the barrel and carefully put the lid on. The barrel of gunpowder was important to Jiefang and he was going to use it well. He already thought about the happiness this barrel of gunpowder brought to him. It will ignite his homemade gun and make a loud and clear bang in the village, and the other kids will admire him. If others asked him how he got the gunpowder, then he would tell them that he had made it himself, that he had found a way to make gunpowder without using Sulphur. And they would go off crazed to experiment themselves, except they won't find his formula, even in all of their lives.

'I have to hide this barrel well,' Jiefang said to himself, 'I can't bring this barrel to the village; I have to hide it in the ground.'

So Jiefang dug a hole in the mountain, and then he put the metal barrel inside.

Now the shell was empty and Jiefang could sleep inside like the Vietnamese soldier. He used his shirt to clean the mess inside the shell and then climbed inside. It wasn't easy, but he managed to put the other half of the shell back in place. It was pitch-black inside as the bomb came together. The smell of gunpowder was still strong, but the smell just made Jiefang feel at peace, as if there was a calming agent hidden in the gunpowder. As Jiefang was lying in the shell, he felt everything in the world far from him, and a sense of warmth came over his body. He could imagine US fighter-planes roaming the skies without even needing to close his eyes. He imagined them throwing down countless bombs, exploding all around, and Jiefangfelt safe. Sometimes Jiefang thought that he himself was a bomb, too, flying in the sky. Lying inside the bomb, Jiefang found that he no longer had his idiotic smile anymore.

The bomb had now become Jiefang's other home. Jiefang would run up the mountain every chance he got and would make his way into it like a squirrel. He had moved quite a lot from the village to the top of the mountain. He took a few things from the village, including five bullets, his homemade gun, and his Young Pioneer's red scarf (Jiefang had two red scarves; the old one was around his neck, and a new one), a set photo from the model opera *Shajiabang*, eight comic books, one pulley, a blanket and a radio that was about as big as a book. This was the village's only radio. It belonged to Jiefang's father. Ever since the first time that Jiefang's father was taken, his Pa had never listened to the radio again. His Pa was melancholic all day, deep in thought. Jiefang saw that a thick layer of dust had settled on the radio at the front of the bed and so he moved the radio inside the bomb. He guessed that his father wouldn't be interested in the radio right now and wouldn't know that he had taken it.

Jiefang placed these things in different corners inside the bomb as he was used to putting things away in an orderly manner. He had always been someone who was tidy. He turned on the radio lying inside the bombshell. The radio played nothing, it just made some strange noises. He thought maybe the radio was broken, and he tried it outside of the bomb and the radio still worked. He guessed that the bombshell blocked the radio-waves. Jiefang was extremely put off by the fact that he couldn't get the stations from Beijing or Shanghai inside the bomb.

No matter what, it felt comforting to Jiefang to make a home inside the bomb. This was a place of darkness and as long as he crawled inside, he will be swallowed by it. Jiefang felt calm from the smell of gunpowder still inside the bombshell. The shell was small, yet the dark-ness made it seem like it had no borders, it seemed to expand out.

Lying in the shell, Jiefang felt that reality was far, far away from him. Sometimes he even thought that the shell was floating above reality. He felt so relaxed and happy inside the shell. He would smile his idiotic smile in school or in the village, but inside the shell, he would no longer smile idiotically. He didn't understand what was behind this.

Half of the shell was buried in the mud, so it was cool even during summer. The school and the village were like special tunnels used only to pass along heat, and the village was so hot it burned. The children would spend their time in the village river, with only their heads above water. The black heads bobbing in the river were like maggots squirming in the manure pit. Jiefang didn't go to the river and instead, he went to the shell after school. Now, he was able to slip in and out of the shell, and he felt his body was as soft as a squirrel's.

One day, Radish bumped into Jiefang at the head of the village after a few days incapable of finding him, so he asked him what he was up to. Jiefang was just in the process of running up the mountain. He stopped to talk to Radish because he didn't want Radish to follow him. He didn't want anyone to find his hiding space. Radish was observing Jiefang and he discovered that Jiefang did look foolish, and when he smiled he looked like an idiot. The children were talking about how Jiefang had been disappearing mysteriously the last few days, and they even said that he had turned into a squirrel going up and down the mountain. Radish looked at Jiefang's eyes and found that his eyes were really red, and he really did look like a squirrel. *Had he really turned into a squirrel?*

A child ran out from a far alleyway. Then a whole group of children followed. The child at the front of the pack was the son of Youshan, of the 'four bad elements.' He was so skinny, and he looked like a weed in the wind as he ran.

The children behind him were stronger, and they chased and beat up Youshan's son. The adults in the village were allowed to discipline the 'four bad elements' and so the children thought they could discipline the children of the 'four bad elements' at will, too. Yet, they only beat up Youshan's son. Youshan's son had a strange phobia about noises; whenever he heard something loud, he thought someone was about to beat him, and so he would run with his head covered. The children were fascinated with him as long as he did this, and they'd often want to beat him.

When the kids had caught up to Youshan's son, they surrounded him and started to torture him. Some of them kicked the child and others threw their pee at him, and some even wanted the kid to eat cow dung. Youshan's son cried until his throat hurt, except his cries sounded fake. They didn't come from his throat and there was no substance in them –no pain, and no spirit.

In the past, Strongbull would have vigorously participated, but now he stood to one side, watching. Strongbull looked over at Jiefang and Radish, who were not far. He saw that Jiefang was watching them, smiling idiotically.

Jiefang suddenly had a headache. When he saw violence, the scene of his own beating would float up in front of him. He would see the blood that looked like a flower spraying out of the top of his head. This would happen every time he saw fights after being injured by Strongbull. He would always get a headache as if the kids were hitting *him* on the head. He couldn't stay there any longer because of his headache and because he felt faint. He turned and ran. Radish didn't know what had happened to Jiefang, and Jiefang disappeared quickly into the woods. As he disappeared into the woods, Radish thought about how he looked exactly like a squirrel.

At last, Jiefang was inside the shell again; the cool place that was also warm, the cave where the darkness expanded without limit, this secret place, this place that comforted him. The scene of Youshan's son's beating flashed before Jiefang's eyes but now Jiefang no longer had a headache. Perhaps it was because he had run so fast, but he was tired and so he closed his eyes. After a while, Jiefang fell asleep. The images from the beating made it into his dreams, but this time he was the one being beaten. Jiefang twisted his body about in the dreams and tears ran down like streams across his face.

His clothes were soaked when he woke up. He was shocked and couldn't remember where he was. He sat up with a jolt and his head banged heavily against the shell, the pain sending sparks through his eyes. He finally understood that he had fallen asleep in the shell. He sighed a sigh of relief when he realised that it had all only been a nightmare. He climbed out of the shell. It was quiet all around and he couldn't hear any human activity. Even birdsong sounded strange right now; it was no longer a bath for the ears, it was sorrowful. He felt the world, once familiar, beginning to change as he exited the shell. He raised his head to look at the sky and the sun was still in the east. Jiefang glanced once at the sun and he could no longer see anything anymore; darkness had descended on him. Then he remembered the sun was in the west when he had climbed into the shell, so why was it in the east now that he had woken up? He didn't know if time could be turned back, but he knew that he had slept in the shell for at least a day. It could also have been several days.

He had a bad feeling, and he didn't know why. Jiefang squeezed out the tears from his shirt and ran down the mountain. There were big character posters at the village head. Jiefang stopped to read them and their content made him smile his idiotic smile.

The big character poster was directed at Jiefang's father. It said that Jiefang's father had always listened to enemy radio stations in the middle of the night on his radio; not only Capitalist decadent music, but also blue music and propaganda from the reactionaries, and had spread these counter-revolutionary ideas amongst the masses.

So, the big character poster concluded, Jiefang's father was looking forward to Chiang Kai-shek and the KMT to counter-attack the mainland. Jiefang did not believe what the big character poster read. Of course, his father owned the only radio in the village (lots of people were jealous of this), but he had never listened to an enemy station. Jiefang's father had warned him about not listening to enemy stations. *It was fake*, what the big character poster said, *they were making an unfounded attack.*

*

Jiefang wanted to control himself so that he didn't have to smile, but he couldn't do it. So he slapped himself twice across the face. 'You should be crying, not laughing!' he said to himself.

Were your tears used up in your dreams, and you don't know how to cry? After the sound of his slaps, he felt the red hot burn on his face, and he ran home with his hand on his cheek.

As he entered the family courtyard, he saw his Ma sitting dumbly on the threshold, the light went out of her eyes. Her eyes looked dry as if there were no more tears. 'Is Daddy okay?' Asked Jiefang.

When she saw him, she cried out. 'Where have you been? You've been missing for three days and nights. I couldn't find you,' she said.

'Where is Daddy?'

'Your Daddy has been taken again, but don't worry, he will be okay.'

'Why would they take away Daddy?'

She did not reply. Instead she said, 'Jiefang, where the hell have you been the last few days? I've been worried sick. I asked Radish and Radish told me you had turned into a squirrel.'

'Radish's Mum turned into a squirrel.'

'Jiefang, did Strongbull turn your brains into mush? Don't leave anymore, I'm so worried. I'm worried you won't be able to find home.'

Jiefang wanted to ignore his mother. She had started treating him like an idiot as soon as he had been hit. Even though he smiled like an idiot, he wasn't one. Jiefang went towards the barracks. He ran like the wind and at one point, he thought he was flying. Soon, Jiefang had arrived at the barracks. The doors were closed and a bunch of children were trying to peer inside through the crack in the door. They saw Jiefang coming and looked at him with strange eyes. Jiefang knew that his father was inside. Jiefang didn't want to be in the huddle with all the other kids. He went to the window behind the barracks and looked in. He saw Shouren with a cigarette, going around his father again and again with a stick. Shouren always acted this way when he was disciplining someone; he liked to imitate the KMT in the movies as if he were a fighter under the Sino-American Cooperative Organization.

Jiefang climbed up to the highest window ledge and he looked just like a little hen that had flown to the top of the enclosure. The kids came to see what the fuss was behind the house and they giggled, with their heads up, standing underneath the window. Jiefang ignored them. He knew that they were happy in his distress; Strongbull's accomplices always were. It was even possible that Strongbull was the one who asked them to come here to laugh at him.

A child shouted, 'Jiefang! Your dad is done for this time! Not only does he listen to enemy stations, but he is a huge pervert! I heard when he was painting the Mao portrait on Shouren's wall, he entered through the window of Shouren's house and did it with his wife. Your father is a big pervert!'

Jiefang's face dropped. Even though he was smiling, his eyes were not; angry daggers hid there. Jiefang almost rolled off the window and went for the kid who had shouted out. The kid saw what was coming and fled in a hurry. The children knew that Jiefang had a brain problem after Strongbull had hurt him and he had a fearless spirit. He would often charge around like a bull who had been disturbed. The kids were scared of him, of his deliberately upsetting smile.

Jiefang didn't go chase the kid. He went to the door of the barracks and knocked on it repeatedly. 'Open the door!' he shouted.

Shouren, with a cigarette dangling from his mouth, opened the door, and he furrowed his brow when he saw it was Jiefang. No one dared knock on the door when Shouren was interrogating; the only person who dared was an idiot such as Jiefang. Shouren heard Strongbull had cracked open Jiefang's brains and he was stupid now. He didn't know what the idiot wanted from him. 'What are you yelling about?' he said.

'Why have you locked up my Daddy? He painted so many Chairman Mao portraits; why would you lock him up?'

Shouren ignored Jiefang and closed the door with a bang, which hit Jiefang on the head. Jiefang didn't want to give up and wanted to reason with Shouren, so he started banging on the door again. His banging was passionate, but the door didn't open. He knocked for five more minutes.

The door opened suddenly. Shouren's face was as black as coal. 'Is this a rebellion? How old are you? You want to rebel?'

Shouren quickly grabbed Jiefang by the lapels and lifted him up, throwing him on the yard of the barracks. After he hit the ground, white dust floated up all around him. He felt soreness and an ache on his sitting bone. A group of children quickly surrounded him, standing close to him, looking between both Shouren and Jiefang. Radish was among them.

'If you come over here, I'm going to kill you,' said Shouren.

Shouren took a look at the children far away and said again, 'This idiot, children–he is a troublemaker, the son of the newly appointed Counter-Revolutionary. Go ahead, beat him up.'

The children had pure hatred and coldness in their eyes.

This was when Radish came over to Jiefang, 'Jiefang, why don't you leave? They are looking at you. If you don't leave, they might really beat you up.'

The children looked merciless and keen, their gaze piercing Jiefang, just like glass shards that have been embedded into his body; at full attack. Jiefang knew that after what Shouren said, they really would come and attack him. So he scrambled quickly off the ground and ran towards the mountains. Jiefang's shirt flew like a kite, higher than even his head, and then he disappeared into the clouds.

He came to his dark place; a place as warm as a stream warmed in the summer, a safe cove that no one knew about; a cave permeated with the smell of gunpowder where he felt as if he was flying. Jiefang curled up like a mouse, with his head in his shoulders and his back stooped. His hands holding on to his ankles; he had turned himself into a ball. Jiefang didn't know how long he had been lying in the shell, but he didn't want to leave, he was afraid. He closed his eyes and he saw the kids' eyes in the darkness, flying in the sky, like flashing daggers. Jiefang felt the daggers would slice open his skin if he left the shell. He felt himself getting smaller and smaller until he was a ball of water, and then a thread of smoke.

Later, he felt the steam become water again, and the water grew until it was a ball. He felt himself stretch open both his legs in the dark, as well as both his arms. He heard the sounds that he himself had made in the dark, and these sounds started off being afraid and sad, but slowly they had become calm and determined.

If your father really was a Counter-Revolutionary, then your life was over, so you'd better know how to save yourself. You have to become someone amazing, you have to do things that others can't do, and then no one will bully you again.

Jiefang felt excited when he said these words, as if the sound was made by the Leader; he was almost moved to tears. He saw himself climb out of the dark cave and then dig out a stone, brushing away the dirt, and taking out that iron barrel. Inside the barrel was black dynamite. He took out about 500g of dynamite and then buried the iron barrel again.

*

'Jiefang, where are you? Jiefang, where are you?'

Radish heard Jiefang's mother shout for him one night in the village. Radish realised that it had been a few days since he had seen Jiefang. *Where did Jiefang go?* He was curious. Raish was already asleep, but he still got up from his bed, and came to meet Jiefang's mother. He was curious about Jiefang's whereabouts.

'I don't know where he is. He disappeared. In the past, he would disappear for two or three days, but this time it has been over a week. I don't know where he is. Radish, do you know where he is? Do you think something happened to Jiefang?' asked Jiefang's mother.

Radish didn't know where Jiefang was. He thought about everyone else saying that Jiefang would turn into a squirrel and run into the woods. *Maybe they were right*, he thought, *maybe Jiefang really had turned into a squirrel; maybe he was roaming wild all around the mountains. Radish thought it wasn't such a bad thing, becoming a squirrel; it must be an easy life.* Radish didn't tell Jiefang's mother what he thought. He knew that Jiefang's mother would not believe such a thing.

When Radish went past Jiefang's home the next day, he saw that Jiefang's mother was sitting on her doorstep crying. Jiefang's mother said as she cried, 'I have had such a sad life. . . His father sleeps with someone else and is locked up. . . Why is my life so sad? My son has disappeared, I don't even know if he's dead or alive. . .'

Radish was sad listening to this and he thought he should help Jiefang's mother. At least he should try to make her feel better. Radish wordlessly came towards her. 'Have you looked on the mountain? Jiefang is definitely up on the mountain,' he said.

Jiefang's mother was scared; she didn't think that someone would talk to her. Since Jiefang's father had been locked up, very few people purposefully talked to her. She stopped crying and looked at Radish in a begging way, 'Radish, do you know where Jiefang is? You must know where Jiefang is!'

'I don't know. . .But they said. . .They said Jiefang turned into a squirrel. You don't have to believe it, it's just what they told me. They saw Jiefang turn into a squirrel and disappear into the woods.'

Jiefang's mother screamed in sorrow, 'Radish, why would you lie to me!? Why would Jiefang turn into a squirrel?'

Radish was confused by her crying, 'I'm not lying to you, why would I do that? It's just what I have been told. . . Don't cry, let's go together into the mountains. Perhaps Jiefang can change back!'

Jiefang's mother looked at Radish and asked, 'You would go with me? Do you know where Jiefang is?'

'I told you, I don't know where he is. I've said this

before, I don't know. I'm not lying to you. But I'll come with you to find him. Don't cry anymore, what's the use in crying?'

After saying this, Radish reached over to hold Jiefang's mother's hand. It looked like Jiefang's mother had no other ideas, so she followed Radish like a child, towards the rows of mountains on the west side of the village. She was full of hope as if she would be able to find Jiefang if she just followed Radish.

As soon as they arrived at the foot of the mountain, Strongbull ran over to them. Strongbull saw Radish take Jiefang's Ma towards the top of the mountain. 'Radish, what the fuck are you doing?' asked Strongbull.

'I'm going with her to find Jiefang.'

'How do you know that Jiefang was on the mountain?'

'They told me that Jiefang had turned into a squirrel. We are going to call on him and ask him to turn back.'

'You're so fucking stupid–that's superstition. How could a human turn into a squirrel?'

Jiefang's mother ignored Strongbull completely. She thought that her son's disappearance had something to do with Strongbull's hit and that Strongbull had made Jiefang stupid, and that's why he had disappeared. But when Jiefang's mother saw Strongbull she still started crying sadly. In recent days, she always wanted to cry. She felt that except for crying, she had nothing else to do.

Strongbull heard Jiefang's mother's crying and turned his head, 'Don't listen to Radish. Jiefang wouldn't turn into a squirrel. Jiefang definitely isn't on the mountain. I've been there with my friends. We've looked all over the mountains and we haven't found Jiefang.'

Strongbull was telling the truth. He really did take the kids to the mountain to look for Jiefang. He was worried when he heard that Jiefang had gone missing. Jiefang had turned strange since he had hit him and now he had disappeared – Strongbull knew it had something to do with him. Now he really wanted to find Jiefang in the mountains. If he could find Jiefang and deliver him to his Ma, Strongbull would feel happy. Yet he couldn't find him. Jiefang wasn't on the mountain. He definitely wasn't on the mountain.

The three of them walked towards the woods. They looked right and left as they worried about losing sight of him if they didn't look thoroughly. It was the height of summer, the leaves of the plants and the weeds were so green they looked black, and the air outside the woods had stagnated, but a cool breeze rushed in and out of the woods, comforting the body. Radish thought that this was a shady kind of breeze and was related to Jiefang in some way.

When he said this to Strongbull, Strongbull kicked him stridently. 'Don't be so fucking mystical,' he said.

Before he had finished his sentence, Radish shouted again, 'Look, a squirrel!'

There it was, a squirrel was looking at them from a tree not far away. The squirrel seemed to know them and was watching them all along. It sniffed as if smelling their scent. Radish thought that its eyes looked familiar, just like Jiefang's wary eyes. Radish was afraid of these thoughts. Then he heard Jiefang's mother cry out, 'Jiefang, Jiefang, is that you? Are you really a squirrel now?'

The squirrel blinked once and disappeared without a trace.

It was as if Jiefang's Ma believed that her son had turned into a squirrel. She cried harder now than anyone else, 'Jiefang, where are you? Come back. Where are you?'

When the squirrel appeared before them again, Radish and Strongbull recognised it. It was a red squirrel with a pelt as red as a flame, its tail high up in the air and a white spot on its forehead. It was the only white on top of its flaming pelt and it was sobering. The squirrel seemed to be constantly following them.

When the squirrel appeared the third time, Radish became afraid. 'Strongbull, look, the squirrel is here again. Perhaps they were right; Jiefang really is a squirrel.'

This time, Strongbull did not speak.

Radish kept showing up at the village head. It had been two months since Jiefang's disappearance. Most of the children in the village had forgotten about him, but not Radish. Radish had the feeling that Jiefang wasn't far from the village and he thought sometimes that Jiefang would suddenly appear in front of him. So, he waited for Jiefang to come back.

Jiefang had told some of the other children about this theory of his, but all he received in return was their merciless mockery. The children took it for granted that Jiefang was no longer in this world. There were some who didn't remember what Jiefang looked like anymore, as if he were a figure from another era. But Radish remembered Jiefang and one day he asked Strongbull, 'Do you think he'll be back one day, Strongbull?'

Radish's question disturbed Strongbull. Jiefang's sudden disappearance made Strongbull feel the certain strangeness of life, as if a part of it had disappeared. He was unable to figure this out and he didn't want to think about it. And so he disliked Radish's question.

'You have a fucking problem,' he said to Radish. 'Why do you care? You're not Jiefang's Ma. Jiefang's Ma has turned into a wailing woman, do you want to become one, too?'

Radish thought it was strange of Strongbull to have

such a big reaction. What the hell?, Radish didn't think he'd become a wailing woman. He was a man. But it was true: There was something wrong with Jiefang's Ma. She had had too many blows–nobody would be able to stand it. Her husband was a newly declared Counter-Revolutionary and he was purged a few times by the revolutionary masses. The authorities also said that he was an enemy spy sent by the KMT. She had turned after this. She looked disabled and others would say that her son was alive, but had turned into a squirrel. But Jiefang's Ma wasn't completely insane yet, she was still working at the production team. She wouldn't be working if she were crazy.

*

Radish was often alone at the head of the village. He saw Strongbull run along the mountain, and he wanted to follow him, but Strongbull was against it. Radish thought it was probably because he would relentlessly bring up Jiefang and Strongbull had gotten tired of it. Then one day, a child told Radish that Strongbull got together with the girl with the long braid and he would bring her to the mountains. Now he knew the real reason Strongbull didn't want him to follow.

Radish was also interested in the girl with the long hair and he was jealous of Strongbull. *If Jiefang knew*, thought

Radish, *he would be jealous, too*. He knew that Jiefang also liked the girl with the long braid. Radish was not surprised by this turn of events at all; Strongbull had seriously discussed this girl with him once when they were above the manure pit taking a shit. As they were discussing her, Strongbull suddenly changed course to say that he had a layer of soft fuzz down below, and he asked if Radish had it, too. Radish flushed and replied, 'No.'

If you looked south from the head of the village, your gaze would arrive at the horizon far away. Not many people would enter your vision because very few people came to this village. Only white clouds came across the horizon, the sparrows flying beneath the white clouds, the green fields, and the streams running in between the fields, the poplars and willows next to the streams, and the winding farming roads that connected the edge of the horizon with the rest of the world. . .

One day, some black dots appeared on the horizon. Radish's heart started racing. He felt like something was about to happen. In the past, there would only be one or two black spots on the horizon, unlike a whole host of them that had now appeared. Radish climbed on to the tree and gazed to the south. He looked closer and saw that it was a unit marching, and the unit seemed to have good news, because he heard the sounds of drums and gongs. It was true, the sounds of gongs started to get louder and as the unit was walking along the windy roads, it was getting closer and closer to the village.

The other children also heard the sound of the gongs. They climbed on to trees and perched on the branches like birds. They tried to guess where the unit had come from. Now, Radish, who had clambered on to the fragrant camphor tree, started screaming loudly, 'Jiefang! It's Jiefang! Jiefang is on a stretcher with a big red flower pinned to his chest!'

The other children also saw Jiefang. They felt like they were dreaming as they weren't quite used to seeing Jiefang all of a sudden. The unit finally walked into the village. It was true, it was Jiefang who was on the stretcher, with a big red flower pinned to his chest. There were bandages on both his head and his foot, just like the KMT soldiers' in the movies after a defeat. A golden walking stick lay next to Jiefang. The children didn't know what had happened to Jiefang, they just saw a brilliant smile on his face and not the idiotic one. There was a satisfaction in his smile that was not describable. Jiefang started to wave to the children when he was still far away and he looked just like a magnificent hero. The stretcher-bearers and gong-hitters were all adults, and their smiles were just as magnificent. They all looked as if they had just launched a man-made satellite around Earth.

The unit walked towards the barracks under Jiefang's direction. The children followed. The children had guessed by now that Jiefang had done something amazing while he was gone otherwise, they wouldn't have brought him home with gongs and drums. But the children didn't express too much warmth and they didn't not react when Jiefang waved at them. Their benevolence was related to Jiefang's father, who had recently been labelled a Counter-Revolutionary. They didn't want to cheer on a Counter-Revolutionary's son. However, it was as though they had no emotions either, because they were still curious as to what Jiefang had done. It wasn't long before they were at the barracks.

The stretcher was already on the floor and Jiefang got up from it. He could only stand firm with the help of the golden walking stick. One of his legs, which was wrapped in bandages, was obviously shorter than it used to be. The children guessed that Jiefang's leg was broken. Three of the outsiders, who had serious but sincere expressions, went into the barracks' office. Jiefang peeked into the room now and again, looking deeply worried. The sound of gongs did not stop and the unit was still hitting them with force standing on the grounds of the barracks. The villagers had all run towards the sound of the gongs and they were very shocked when they saw Jiefang. It was as if Jiefang knew that they would look like this upon seeing him, and he ignored everyone, pretending he no longer knew who the people in the village were.

The three outsiders came out of the office after a while and their expressions had completely changed; their seriousness and sincerity had disappeared. Their faces had turned dark as if they had just been the victims of a huge con. Shouren, who came out with them, also had a dark face. One of the outsiders waved to the drum and gong-hitters, telling them to stop. Then he said, 'Let's go.'

Jiefang's mother had gotten to them now. She looked manic and threw herself at Jiefang like a hungry leopard, like she was going to eat him. She had already heard that Jiefang had lost a leg and here he was being brought on a stretcher. She held on to his shorter leg and shouted, 'What happened to you, Jiefang? How did you get like this? Where's the rest of your leg?'

Before Jiefang had a chance to reply, Jiefang's mother had scrambled to the outsiders, holding on to the one at the front. She shouted out, 'What did you do to him? He's just a child! Where is the rest of his leg? Where is it?'

All the outsiders turned pale. They understood the passionate response of a mother. They knew this was going to happen when they brought the child home and they had hoped that the honour they had put on him would salve the parents' sadness. But that didn't look possible now. There was no such thing as comfort in this village. The child's father was a

Counter-Revolutionary. It was impossible that the son of a Counter-Revolutionary would be a hero. Jiefang's mother had a grip on the outsiders, who didn't know what to do. Jiefang suddenly shouted at his mother, 'What do you think you're doing? Why are you making trouble?'

Everyone had quietened down, watching Jiefang. Shouren, with nonchalance, said to the masses and children on the grounds, 'Go away, don't you have work to do? There's nothing to see here.'

Shouren was dispersing the crowds. Jiefang's gaze followed him. And suddenly tears came pouring out of him.

Jiefang walked back to the village with his walking stick. Children were always following him from afar. Jiefang heard them giggle and laugh and thought ill of their silliness; *This is not the attitude to have towards a hero.* He wanted to run towards them and tell them what amazing deed he had done, but he stopped himself. He needed to wait for a formal situation, at an assembly in the village or the school, when they will honour him as a serious hero. He thought that his heroic status was enough to give a presentation at assembly.

Radish was gloating; Jiefang was finally back. This proved that Radish's instincts were right. Radish started boasting in front of the other children, 'You didn't believe me, but I told you Jiefang would come back.'

But Radish did not know what Earth-shattering feat Jiefang did in the days that he had been missing, and one day he asked Jiefang. Jiefang answered proudly, 'Wait for my report.'

'Where are you giving the report?'

'Maybe in the village or the school.'

But nothing happened in the village over the next few days. Jiefang started to panic.

Things didn't develop in the way that Jiefang had hoped. People seemed to be indifferent to his return. Jiefang kept up the seriousness befitting of a hero. Even though he would still unconsciously smile idiotically, there was pride and dignity in that smile. The children all knew now that Jiefang was going to give a presentation, but they didn't know if the village or the school would arrange for it to happen. If the school or the village arranged for Jiefang to give a presentation, then it would show that he was a real hero. If they didn't, then Jiefang was just the son of a Counter-Revolutionary, and he was worthless. And this was why Jiefang was in such a panic because he knew that this was what the children thought.

Jiefang saw a few students begin to clean the old and dilapidated auditorium at the school and some of the other students were taking chairs inside. Later, they also took a machine into the auditorium. Jiefang didn't know what kind of machine it was, but he guessed that it might be an audio amplifier.

Jiefang was suddenly so excited; he assumed that

they were preparing for a presentation. Perhaps they were even preparing for him. Perhaps the balding principal will soon invite him to go over and give his speech.

Jiefang went inside the auditorium wrapped by feelings of joy all over his body, which almost made him spin. He suppressed his excitement and returned to the classroom, waiting patiently for the summons. He imagined what he looked like giving a presentation. He even saw rays of light shooting out of his body. He started to giggle, out loud, uncontrollably.

Jiefang was disappointed that still, by nightfall, no one had come to ask for him. He went to go look in the auditorium and realised that they were showing a film called *Breaking with Old Ideas.*

I can't wait for them to arrange it, I have to go ask for it. He had the right to ask for it after he had done something so impressive. So Jiefang decided to go to the office of the bald principal to have a serious talk.

The principal was shocked that Jiefang had shown up. Except he could tell immediately what Jiefang was doing there. The students had already told him; they said that Jiefang wanted to do a presentation at the school. The principal had no idea that Jiefang would come to find him. He knew however that this student had turned extremely stubborn when his head had been hit; and that he would often do unintelligible deeds.

Jiefang sat down in front of the principal. There seemed, hidden in his idiotic smile, a great will.

'Do you need something?' asked the Principal.

'I want to do the presentation. I want to present to the students.'

The principal leaned back and looked at Jiefang, it was as if Jiefang looked younger than he suspected. *This has got to be a superbly intelligent rut*, thought the principal. *Not one student would dare be so immodest.* The principal suddenly started to show interest in the person in front of him. He had heard that in order to be a hero, this child had blown broken his own leg. And so, the principal wanted to know what happened, 'Jiefang, you want to give a presentation? Why don't you give me one first?'

'I want to tell all the students, not just you.'

'How could I grant you a presentation to the students if you don't tell me your heroic deed first?'

'Didn't you see the unit bring me home hitting gongs and beating drums? Would they bring me home like this if I wasn't a hero?'

The principal had nothing to say. *Stubborn people have their own logic, and this logic makes its own sense, it's hard to argue with them.* The principal suddenly lost his interest. 'Then let's forget it if you don't want to talk about it. Why don't you leave?'

Jiefang didn't leave; he stood there with a walking

stick, unmoving like a metal tower. He looked at the principal angrily and said, 'Fine, I'll tell you roughly. Except I won't tell you everything. I will only say everything when I am giving the students the presentation.'

The principal smiled indifferently and said, 'Do whatever you want.'

The principal's indifference affected Jiefang, who didn't know where to start. He opened his mouth but didn't know where to begin, as if he suddenly lost the ability to speak.

'What's wrong, Jiefang?'

'I don't know where to start.'

'Let me ask you questions then, how does that sound?'

Jiefang looked straight at the principal and did not make a stance.

'I heard that your leg was broken by the time-bomb buried under the train tracks, is that true?'

'It is.'

'Who buried the time bomb?'

'I don't know… but it must have been a Counter-Revolutionary.'

'How did you find it?'

'I was walking along the railroad when I heard a tick-tock of a clock; later I realised it was a time-bomb. It was class enemies doing destruction by burying it under the train track.'

'So, you dug it out.'

'Yes, but when I touched the bomb, it exploded.' Jiefang lost patience when he said this, and he furrowed his brow. 'I fainted, and when I woke up, I discovered I was in the hospital. They told me that I was a hero. They said that the bomb had blown up the train tracks and also my leg. I had saved the lives of everyone on the train because the operator knew that an accident had happened ahead and stopped. They said I was a hero. I know that anyone would do this if they were in the same situation and what I had done is minor. But they called me a hero.' Jiefang said all this quickly.

Jiefang didn't look at the principal at all when he was speaking. The principal's sunken eyes were sharp yet suspicious; Jiefang didn't like his eyes. Jiefang knew that the principal's eyes were like two sorry flies circling him. Jiefang knew that the principal did not believe him.

The principal cleared his throat and changed the topic, 'Why did you leave home? Where have you been? Circling around the railroad?'

Jiefang flushed. He didn't want to answer his boring questions.

But the principal had more, 'Were you at the railroad?' The principal asked.

Jiefang was annoyed by these questions, 'What do you mean?' He asked.

'What do you think I mean?'

Jiefang looked up at the principal and at his arrogant

face. He really wanted to punch that face as he had already lost his patience with the principal. Except he endured his interrogation and was silent for a while.

'I told you everything,' said Jiefang after some time. 'Are you going to let me give the presentation now?'

'Why don't you leave? We'll have to discuss it.'

'You have to keep your word.'

'You know that this is hard to do, Jiefang. We need to let the superiors decide if you're a hero.'

'Are you fucking with me to make yourself happy?' Jiefang was mad.

The principal hardened, and in a high voice he said, 'You are speaking to a teacher right now, Jiefang.'

Jiefang's face got more and more stern, and both his lips quivered. Suddenly he lifted up the metal walking stick and hit the principal straight on the head.

*

Now Jiefang still loved to lie inside the dark bomb-shell; this was the only way he felt calm, away from reality. The villagers didn't really think that he was a hero and they didn't want him to give a presentation. Everyone knew about him hitting the principal. The children discussed this in groups. Their expressions were strange and exaggerated as if Jiefang was a mystery that they couldn't figure out. They were even more curious about Jiefang and in their looks towards him, there was a cold inquiry, as if he was an ant under a magnifying glass.

Jiefang went to his base, inside his shell. But he felt his heart beat uncomfortably even as he sat there; it beat so fast it almost flew out of his chest. He breathed fast and he heard the heaviness of his breathing inside the shell. It sounded just like a northwest wind blowing outside in the winter gloom. He closed his eyes and imagined he was giving a presentation on the auditorium stage, and there were students all around. Then he heard the sound of his own voice and that was when he realised that he was talking to himself in the darkness of the shell.

Even though he was using his presenting tone, he was really just speaking to himself. Yet Jiefang couldn't stop, he kept on talking. The thoughts of the presentation lingered over the past few days and he felt like he would collapse if he didn't get them all out. Soon he was able to get out the whole speech. He heard applause, a tide of applause, from underneath the auditorium. He cried immediately. He no longer felt panicked, and his breathing returned to normal. He slipped out from the dark shell.

*

It seemed that Jiefang had distanced himself from all the other children.

He discovered that they would walk behind him, affecting a limp–even Radish. He had wanted to chase after them and hit them with his metal walking stick, but thought that he couldn't catch them, so gave up. Even though he had a crippled foot, it was still useful, because at least now he had a metal weapon. If he didn't have this metal weapon, perhaps they would have bullied him the same way they had the other children of the 'four evil elements.'

Jiefang walked towards the mountain. Just as it was described in *Fighting North and South*, someone with a walking stick can climb very fast. Soon, the children could no longer see him.

Jiefang had developed a habit that he couldn't control. He spoke loudly when there was no one around, like he was giving a presentation. Not only did he do it involuntarily inside the shell, but he would do this alone in the woods, too. He would want to speak whenever there was no one around, until he could vehemently finish the presentation.

One day, Jiefang looked around him and saw no one around, so he started to talk. He heard someone call him from behind as soon as he started. It sounded like Radish. He didn't want anyone to see him give a presentation and so he stopped talking. His face flushed red because it took persistence to endure not talking.

'What are you doing here?'

'I heard someone speaking, so I came over. Jiefang, who were you talking to? Why were you speaking so loudly? Jiefang, were you giving a presentation? Were you practicing?'

'I don't need to practice.'

'Jiefang, why don't you give up? They're not going to let you give a presentation at the school!'

Jiefang said nothing.

'Why do you have to give a presentation at the school? If you wanted to give a presentation, you can. . . Let's do it, Jiefang, I want to hear your story, why don't you give the presentation to me? They said you got injured when you were digging out a time-bomb. Is that right?'

Jiefang suddenly was itchy all over and the desire to perform overtook him. He started to laugh idiotically and as he laughed, his eyes got misty.

'Tell me about it, Jiefang.'

Jiefang stood in front of Radish, preparing to launch into words. Yet he was speechless again and couldn't say anything. He opened his mouth and there was a painful yet strange smile on his face.

The children all knew Jiefang wanted to give them a presentation and now they knew that Jiefang couldn't speak a word in front of them. They had a new way and method for mocking Jiefang. They followed behind Jiefang, shouting loudly, 'Jiefang, Jiefang! Give us a presentation!'

When they teased like this, their faces were as happy as if they had found gold coins. They also didn't forget to walk like Jiefang. They looked like toys with springs, the way they staggered about. Jiefang knew people were mocking him. *They are getting bolder and bolder,* Jiefang thought, *They started by talking about me behind my back, and now they are openly mocking me, so soon they'll start to attack me. What should I do?*

One day, Jiefang's mother found that the children were bullying him, so she charged over. 'Strongbull made him stupid, and he broke his leg. You don't feel sorry for him, but you mock him?' She called loudly.

Afterwards, she wailed infernally, 'Lord! It's not fair!'

The children were confused by Jiefang's mother, and soon they awoke to this realisation: She was just the wife of the new Counter-Revolutionary, so she didn't have the right to reprimand him. They gathered around Jiefang's mother and used revolutionary slogans against her. Someone even pushed her. Jiefang's mother knew that the situation was bad, and immediately lost her nerve, shrank into a ball and looked just like a startled rabbit.

Jiefang witnessed all of this from the mountain. Without hesitation, he ran down the moment he saw them push his mother to the ground. He lost his balance because of how fast he had acted, and so in the end, he rolled down the hill like a rubber ball. He lifted the metal stick and ran towards the children. The children saw what was happening and dispersed like flies. Jiefang's eyes were filled with empty and painful tears.

Jiefang's mother stood up from the ground and attempted to hold him. Jiefang got away from her and started up the mountain, limping.

'Jiefang! What are you doing on the mountain? You can't run away!'

*

Jiefang walked on the mountain. The sky was azure blue and his body felt lighter as he saw this blue sky, as if it had a huge attraction to him, and it might suck him away. *What would I become if I were to be sucked into the sky? Maybe I would turn into a cloud, or maybe a streak of blue smoke.* At some point, he even thought that he might fly, but he realised he couldn't leave the ground. He could only dream inside the dark shell. *Maybe it wouldn't be so bad to turn into a white cloud or blue smoke,* he thought.

Now Jiefang lay inside the shell once again. He wanted to always lie like this. He knew that if he didn't leave the shell then he might really become a white cloud or a puff of blue smoke. Some said that after someone died, their soul would turn to blue smoke and go up to the skies. Others said that there were no souls, no blue smoke, only a cold corpse. But if he climbed out of the shell, they would indefinitely harass him. The children would mark him the way they marked trees with their signature, and he would turn into an imperfect tree. Except he already felt that way.

It was up to one organ whether he would climb outside: his stomach. The feeling of hunger would leave a mark on your body and your psyche. The feeling of hunger will make your stomach hot, and your thoughts will concentrate on that organ involuntarily as if there was a knife that was cutting at every nerve. Jiefang couldn't handle it and so he climbed out of the darkness.

Jiefang felt a sense of newness with everything when he climbed out as if he had been in the shell for over a thousand years. He didn't realise the trees and weeds were so green before; it was as if he could see green liquid in the leaves. The colour of the bugs flying in the forests was so bright like someone had just painted it on. When in the past he thought the mud had a rotting smell, now the smell was warm and fresh, just like the smell of newly-fermented rice wine. He greedily sucked all this up. He looked for things to eat in the woods. There were all sorts of colours in his stomach, he felt as if all that he saw had entered his stomach, like eyes were growing out of his stomach.

He found a potato and ate it. After his stomach had the feeling of real food, the walls of his stomach started to move lightly. He heard his stomach sing. What was the song? 'The East is Red?' The song gave people a sense of time; every time the field loudspeaker played this song I would become angry because it was time to eat. 'Sailing the Seas Depends on the Helmsman?' The song was full of gratitude and optimism. 'The rain nourished the cereal seedlings,' it was all about the hope of harvest and seemed to have something to do with the stomach. 'Red Rice and Pumpkin Soup?' What was this folk song about? You can tell from the song title that it has something to do with the stomach. Perhaps the production of these songs had something to do with hunger; the ones composing the songs were familiar with hunger; when their stomachs happily jerked around because it was full of food, they composed these songs according to the rhythm of their stomachs. Who knew?

Jiefang walked in the woods, thinking irrational thoughts. At that moment his brain was over-active and he thought of everything. It was as if he were drunk, he was so excited. But something happened soon after and impacted him. His excitement turned immediately to sadness.

Jiefang saw, in the depths of the woods, Strongbull and the girl with the long braid. They were holding hands singing a song. It was 'The Hero's Song:'

Why is the battle-flag so beautiful; the blood of heroes has stained her

Why is Spring abound; the life of the heroes blossom…

Strongbull didn't like to sing; he didn't have a good voice and when he sang he sounded like a bull. But right now, Strongbull was happy singing, with his expression smiling gladly. Jiefang felt strange seeing this. He felt strange because Strongbull had always bullied that girl and now they were sitting together, holding hands. Jiefang also liked the girl, how wonderful it would be if he could hold the girl's hand!

Were they together? When did this happen?, Jiefang couldn't believe that he hadn't remembered this girl, who had a long braid just like Li Tiemei, the character in the opera. Jiefang had always thought of her in the past. Her long plait warmed him. Once Jiefang saw her wash her hair near the river; hair loose, like a black waterfall. He felt as if the waterfall fell into his heart and made it itch. Jiefang would watch her from afar, but he never spoke to her. He would want to protect her when Strongbull bullied her, he wanted to fight with Strongbull. She was the reason he and Strongbull didn't get along. But now she was holding Strongbull's hand and he had always bullied her. Jiefang couldn't understand this. Maybe Strongbull forced her to act this way. This got Jiefang's attention. Jiefang started to stare at the end of the girl's braid.

Then, he saw her with Strongbull on different occasions. He found that she looked for Strongbull and Strongbull wasn't forcing her. Jiefang would follow behind them with his walking stick, feeling jealous. He saw himself walking with a limp in his mind and felt as if Strongbull, and that girl, acted like his mirror, reflecting his disabled state. Jiefang felt his body reassembling and the phantom part of his leg started hurting again, and soon his heart started to hurt, too.

The pain in his body has not disappeared. Even now as he was lying inside the shell, he still felt the pain of the phantom leg growing. The sense of pain grew like roots from his leg, spreading into space. This painful tree took up the entire shell. He knew that he had a disabled body but he hadn't realised that he had a real problem with it until now. He saw his body turn into a cloth with missing pieces. He felt completely broken by something.

If Strongbull and the girl were a mirror to Jiefang, then he wanted to smash it. It was constantly provoking him—this was his only thought. Jiefang thought perhaps he wasn't good enough for the girl, but neither was Strongbull.

Strongbull was a bully, and how could such a hooligan be good enough for her? Radish had told Jiefang once that, when he and Strongbull were together, they constantly talked dirty, and Strongbull had taken Radish to spy on girls while they showered.

How could such a dirty boy be good enough for her? Jiefang decided that he must speak to this girl; he thought that she should leave Strongbull. She should know that she was a fresh flower, whereas Jiefang was cow-dung.

Why would Strongbull be good enough for her?

Next time, Jiefang stopped the girl at the foot of the mountain. She looked at him with afraid eyes. The girl didn't know why Jiefang had stopped her; everybody had talked about how Jiefang had gone mad.

'You don't need to be afraid, I'm not going to do anything to you. I only wanted to tell you something,' said Jiefang.

'What do you need to tell me?'

'I know what you're in a hurry to do. But I need to tell you, it's not worth it.'

The girl flushed. 'What are you talking about,' she said. 'I'm just going up the mountain for fun.'

'I know someone's waiting for you up there. You don't need to lie to me, nor can you lie to me.'

'Why would I lie to you?'

'You shouldn't be with Strongbull, He's terrible. He's a hooligan and he's a scoundrel.'

The girl flushed harder. She held her plait with both hands and lowered her head.

'I'm not going to lie to you. Strongbull is not good enough for you. He says extremely dirty things, and he secretly watches women shower. He also touches women's tits when you're watching movies. He doesn't have any shame,' said Jiefang.

The girl suddenly started to cry, 'What are you trying to do to me, telling me these things?'

When the girl cried, Jiefang's heart warmed. He jumped towards her, wanting to take care of her. He slapped her on the back; his heart trembling when his hand touched her braid. Then he started shaking as if he had gotten a serious illness and started stroking her plait. She shouted out, 'What are you doing!?'

She escaped him quickly. He followed her.

'Why are you running? Why are you running? I'm caring for you. I know I'm not good enough for you, but Strongbull is worse,' he said.

Jiefang shouted and followed. He accidentally fell. When he got up, he saw someone standing in front of him. It was Strongbull. Strongbull was smiling coldly at Jiefang, 'What the fuck is wrong with you? What were you thinking?'

'I am speaking to her; it has nothing to do with you.'

'You are an ugly frog who wants to eat fresh meat. Why don't you take a look in the mirror? How can you compete with me?'

Jiefang was so angry when he heard this, he took

his walking stick and aimed at Strongbull. Strongbull ducked and took hold of Jiefang's walking stick.

'I don't fight with the disabled. I told myself that I wouldn't fight with you anymore after I hit you that one time. I know that you've had bad luck and I feel sorry for you. But don't push your luck. Don't get on the wrong side of me.'

After Strongbull said this, he swatted away the walking stick and left. He went to the girl, who was crying nearby, to look after her. Then he took the girl's hand and they disappeared from view. Jiefang picked up the walking stick and went towards them.

For a while, Jiefang's mind was empty, with only Strongbull's disapproving face in front of him. His face was just like a dark cloud. He stood there dully and smiled his idiotic smile. He knew how disgusting and pitiful he looked. He slapped himself across the face and said, 'Still fucking smiling!'

It was already the beginning of autumn and though it was near sunset, the sunlight stretched long and bright, and it was full of heat. Jiefang sat on the shell looking around him. The light shone all around him as if there were endless mirrors on the trees. The flapping of the birds' wings and their birdsong were still filling the woods. And not far in the fields, two young calves were fighting, blood strewn over their faces. Their blood-red reproductive organs on the side. Some kids watched the commotion and Jiefang didn't know which calf would win.

Slowly, Jiefang started thinking again. He said involuntarily, 'I know I have failed. I am no longer Strongbull's opponent. My body is gone and I know how they treat the disabled; they won't call me by my name anymore, they'll just call me 'that cripple.' They'll also call me idiot, retard and small Counter-Revolutionary. They will call me this for life. I failed. I thought they were going to make me a hero, but it might not be possible. They just think that I'm pitiable.'

The two calves were fighting each other, one of them was on the ground, and the other didn't want to give him up, and with force used its sharp horns to get at the other. Jiefang saw the hopelessness in the eyes of the calf on the floor. In his mind, the image of Strongbull laughing appeared again. The face was like a sword in his chest, slowing his breathing. 'I can't fight him anymore, I might be able to beat him if I had a good leg, beat him like the hopeless calf, but now I can no longer do that. He doesn't need a lot to defeat me. There is no fairness in this world, now he can be with the girl, holding hands, now that I'm like this.'

I won't let him get away from it, let him laugh, he won't have long left.

'I'm not going to let him get away with this,' Jiefang said to himself, 'I won't let him off even if I can't win a fight against him. Unless he suddenly disappears in front of me, unless he is blown away by the wind, otherwise, I'm not going to get rid of him. He's my only enemy on this Earth.'

But Jiefang didn't know where his hate for Strongbull came from. He searched his memory but couldn't remember why he hated Strongbull so much. Besides, the time he hit him on the head, Strongbull actually didn't really harm Jiefang, he just hated him anyway. He hated him so much.

The day was about to end. It was getting darker, and nothing was visible anymore. The villages afar lit their lights. Jiefang stood there, not moving.

He couldn't get rid of Strongbull's mocking face, as if his smile was hidden in every leaf. These smiles had blocked his oesophagus and he couldn't breathe. It made him angry.

'Laugh all you want! It won't be for long anyway,' he screamed.

Time was passing slowly. He watched the moon rise, moving from one side of the tree branches to the next. He stood up and walked to the stone plate next to the shell. There was a can of dynamite underneath, black TNT.

He picked up the stone and the smell of the dynamite entered his nostrils like strong spirit. He felt his body grow; his lungs, his heart and his blood boiling. He said suddenly to the smiling face in front of him, 'Let's see how long you can be happy for.'

*

In the evening, the villagers were woken by the sound ran towards the sound.

They found that the attic at Strongbull's house had disappeared. Strongbull's parents did not sleep in the attic, so they were fine, but Strongbull was nowhere to be seen. Strongbull's parents looked for their son in the debris, but couldn't find him, as if he had gone into the skies. At last, the town policemen found Strongbull. He was lying about 100 meters from his home, on the grass, a bloody pie. He was taken to the hospital.

*

Jiefang disappeared again that morning. Everybody linked the explosion with Jiefang. The police even issued an arrest warrant for him. Yet, Jiefang disappeared. After a month, Strongbull came out of the hospital. Part of his leg was gone and he had a walking stick like Jiefang, except his was made from wood. The people in the village couldn't find Jiefang and neither could the police. They reckoned that this time Jiefang had disappeared for good, but Jiefang's mother still stood at the village head, waiting for her son's sudden return.

As for the bomb's origin, the police asked Jiefang's parents about it many times and didn't get any results. The origin of the bomb and Jiefang's disappearance became a mystery.

One day, Radish and Strongbull went to play in the mountains. They talked on and off. Then, they talked about Jiefang.

'Where did his bomb come from, do you think, Strongbull?'

'I don't know.'

'Why did Jiefang want to bomb your home?'

'I don't know, maybe to revenge me. He hated me after I hit him.'

'He turned strange after you hit him, don't you think he's strange?'

'Yes.'

'After you hit him, he went up to the mountain constantly. They said he turned into a squirrel, too.'

'Who knows.'

'They also said Jiefang was responsible for dynamite on the railways and that he had blown off his own leg.'

'I didn't know that.'

They both saw the squirrel jumping in front of them, and the squirrel looked back at them repeatedly. Radish recognised the squirrel as the same one he saw the first time they went to search for Jiefang. It had a white patch on his head, he could tell just by glancing at it. They followed the squirrel. The squirrel was neither fast nor slow and kept its distance from them. They followed it for a long time on the mountain.

'Look, Strongbull, the squirrel knows who we are, maybe he really is Jiefang.'

'I don't know.'

Radish tripped and fell to the ground. The squirrel went into the woods quickly and disappeared. Radish didn't know what had tripped him and when he lifted some vines, he found a huge piece of metal. Radish screamed.

Hearing Radish's scream, Strongbull turned and saw him knocking on the piece of metal. Strongbull knocked it a few times with his walking stick as well, and the metal made some heavy sounds. Their hearts started to beat quickly and they realised that they were about to make a huge discovery. They didn't say anything. Within a short while, they had taken away the mud on all four sides of the metal and a huge bombshell appeared in front of them.

Someone had obviously moved this bomb and the screws on the end of the bomb had been picked off. They realised something serious was happening and so they ran towards the village.

They brought people along with them when they

returned to the bomb. The villagers carefully removed the top of the shell. A strange smell entered their nostrils—it was just like over-fermented wine. Everyone looked at the bombshell and they saw a dead boy inside. The corpse was fresh and a red cloth was draped across him. The red cloth was made up of two red scarves. Five yellow stars, drawn from chalk, adorned the red cloth.

More from Penguin. . .

A Story of Friendship and Trauma by Chi Zijian

Ji Lianna passionately tends to her flower garden and avoids looking back at her life with remorse. Xiao'e does not know the first thing about plants and cannot stop thinking about her past. Eighty-year-old Ji Lianna is a child of the Jewish diaspora, and young Xiao'e is not sure whether she is human at all. The two women could not be more different. Yet, in a numbingly cold Harbin flat in an old Russian villa, an unlikely friendship blossoms between them. Soon their dark histories come back to haunt them as they realise they have more in common than just a shared address.

Translated from the Chinese by Poppy Toland